The Secret Lives of Cats and Dogs

written by Jenna Dzefko

illustrated by Susan Hartung

 McGraw-Hill
School Division

New York   Farmington

Bobby Martiello loved animals. By his eighth
birthday, he had two dogs, Max and Ellie, and
two cats, Maggie and Leo. He played with his
pets whenever he could, and he loved them all.

One morning, Bobby came running down the stairs. "Come on outside!" he shouted to the dogs, and then he ran outside. The dogs headed toward the front door after him.

But before they could get outside, Maggie the cat said, "Look at that! They always do everything he tells them to do. I don't think dogs are very smart!"

"Is that what you think?" said Max. "You're wrong! You don't realize how smart we are!"

"What do you mean?" asked Maggie.

"Just go over to the window," he said. "You'll see!" As the dogs ran outside, the cats climbed up on the window ledge to watch.

Bobby threw a ball across the yard, and Max and Ellie ran after it. Ellie grabbed it in her mouth and brought it back to Bobby. Bobby took a dog snack out of his pocket and tossed it to Ellie. "Good girl," he said, rubbing her head.

"It's amazing," Maggie said to Leo, "but those dogs are actually very crafty."

After many more rounds of catch, Bobby and the dogs came back inside. They were all tired and thirsty, so Bobby went into the kitchen to get them water.

"So now you see how smart we really are," said Max to the cats. We got all the exercise we needed, plus some treats! Dogs are smart, probably smarter than cats!"

"Oh, yeah?" said Leo. "Just you wait until we get a chance to prove you wrong!"

After they drank all the water they wanted,
Max and Ellie followed Bobby to the couch.
When all four pets tried to jump up next to him,
Bobby said, "Sorry, Max and Ellie, you got too
dirty outside. Mom won't like you up here on her
clean couch."

The cats climbed up next to Bobby. He
rubbed their fur, and soon they were purring
happily. Bobby was asleep and snoring within
minutes.

"Well," said Leo to the dogs on the floor, "it doesn't take much of a brain to figure out who's smarter now. We're up here on the couch because we keep ourselves clean, while you have to sit on the floor."

"What's that sound you were making?" asked Ellie. "It sounds like you have a motor inside you."

"That's called purring," said Maggie. "It's how we communicate. Bobby likes the sound of it, so he pets us even more. It makes him so relaxed that he falls asleep, and then we really have some fun."

"I thought all you cats did was sleep!" said Max.

"Which isn't very social, you know," Ellie added.

Maggie said, "I know what will solve this once and for all, and we can try it out tonight!"

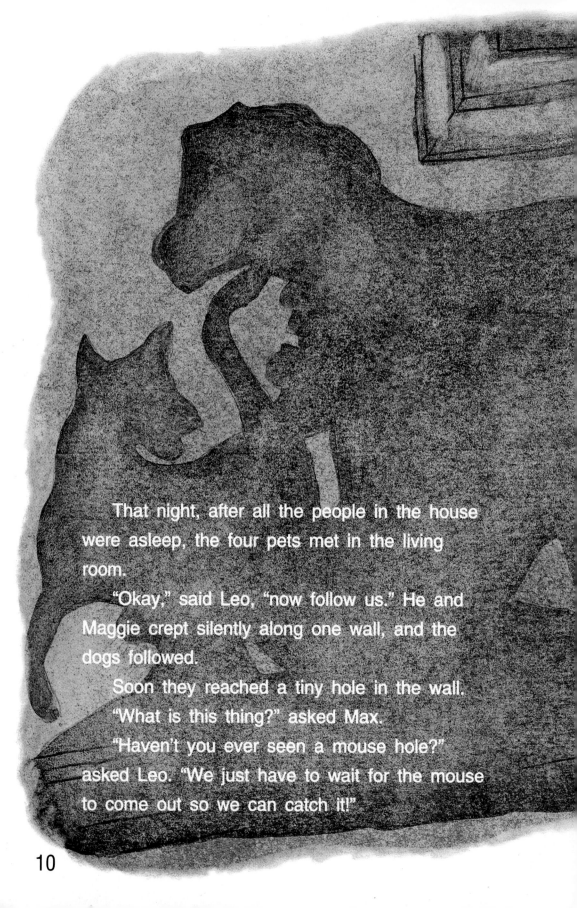

That night, after all the people in the house were asleep, the four pets met in the living room.

"Okay," said Leo, "now follow us." He and Maggie crept silently along one wall, and the dogs followed.

Soon they reached a tiny hole in the wall. "What is this thing?" asked Max.

"Haven't you ever seen a mouse hole?" asked Leo. "We just have to wait for the mouse to come out so we can catch it!"

"But that could take hours!" said Ellie. "We have more important things to do than just wait around here all that time!"

"Well, waiting is just another thing that cats are very good at," Leo explained. "Our job is to keep mice out of the house, whether we wait for them and catch them or scare them away. Catching balls is not anywhere near as important as either one."

Just then, the cats and dogs heard a noise that sounded like it was coming from outside the house.

"What's that?" Maggie asked. She and Leo silently crept over to the front window and peered out. "There's somebody out there!" she hissed.

"Well," said Leo, "what do you think we should do about it?"

"I don't know," said Maggie, flicking her tail.

"I thought cats always had an answer for everything!" Ellie exclaimed.

Maggie looked out the window again. "He seems to be looking for a way to get in!" she reported.

"Leave this one to us," said Max. He and Ellie ran to the door and started barking.

"Hey, that man is running away," Leo called to Maggie. "Their plan is working!"

The two dogs came back into the living room.

"I have to admit that was pretty smart," said Maggie.

Just then Bobby came down the stairs. "Hey, the middle of the night is no time to play!" he said.

"I guess there's more to this whole subject of smartness than we thought," whispered Ellie.

The cats purred and the dogs licked his hand as Bobby petted them all. Suddenly, who was smarter didn't seem to matter at all.